To my mother, Roberta Loomis, and her dreams

C. L.

For Danny, Rama, and little Tomer with love

O. E.

Text copyright © 1997 by Christine Loomis
Illustrations copyright © 1997 by Ora Eitan
All rights reserved. This book, or parts thereof, may not be reproduced in any form
without permission in writing from the publisher. G. P. Putnam's Sons, a division of
The Putnam & Grosset Group, 200 Madison Avenue, New York, NY 10016.
G. P. Putnam's Sons, Reg. U.S. Pat. & Tm. Off. Published simultaneously in Canada
Printed in Hong Kong by South China Printing Co. (1988) Ltd.
Designed by Gunta Alexander. Text set in Friz Quadrata.
The art was done in gouache on plywood panels.

Library of Congress Cataloging-in-Publication Data
Loomis, Christine. Cowboy bunnies / by Christine Loomis; illustrated by Ora Eitan.
p. cm. Summary: Little bunnies spend their day pretending to be cowboys: riding
their ponies, mending fences, counting cows, eating chow, and singing cowboy tunes
until it is time for bed. [1. Cowboys — Fiction. 2. Rabbits — Fiction. 3. Play — Fiction.
4. Stories in rhyme.] I. Eitan, Ora, 1940- ill. II. Title. PZ8.3.L8619Co 1997
[E] — dc20 96-43057 CIP AC ISBN 0-399-22625-7
10 9 8 7 6 5 4 3 2 1 First Impression

COWBOY BUNNIES

Christine Loomis
pictures by Ora Eitan

G. P. Putnam's Sons • New York

Cowboy bunnies
Wake up early
Ride their ponies
Hurly burly

Start at sunup
Work all day
Roping cows
Tossing hay

Mending fences
On the ridges
Jumping gullies
Fixing bridges

Bronco busters
In the saddle
Whoop and holler
Count the cattle

Cowboy bunnies
On the ground
Start the campfire
Gather round

Ring the lunch bell
Rub their bellies
Eat up flapjacks
Eggs and jellies

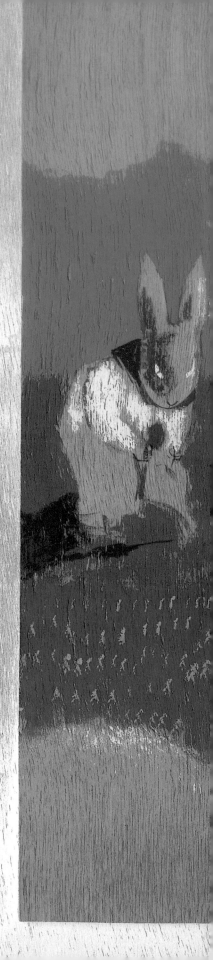

Steak and 'taters   Corn and cake

Bunnies get   A bellyache

Cowboy bunnies
Feeling hot
Find a cool
And shady spot

Chase each other
Sit and doze
Roll their pants up
Dip their toes

Call their ponies
Hit the trail
Over hill
And over dale

Till their work
Is finally done
Then the bunnies
Have some fun

Cowboy bunnies
Big and little
Pick a banjo
Play a fiddle

Grab a partner
Little or big
Dance to the music
Jiggity jig

Sing a lonesome
Cowboy tune
Underneath a
Silver moon

Stay up late   Home they go
Rub their eyes   With sleepy sighs

Cowboy bunnies   In pajamas   Hug and kiss

Their cowboy mamas

Mamas sing
Sweet lullabies
Papas softly
Harmonize

Stars are twinkling
Stars are bright
Cowboy bunnies
Say good night